SOGGY
and the
GOLDEN TREASURE

mabecron books

For those children who find it a little more difficult
to get things done

London Borough of Southwark	
D	
SK 2332952 1	
Askews & Holts	29-Mar-2013
JF	£6.99

SOGGY
and the
GOLDEN TREASURE

Philip Moran

illustrated by

Michael Foreman

It was a glorious day at the high end of summer and Grandfather had gone fishing. Jack and Soggy decided to spend the day at a local farm watching the men bring in the harvest.

They hitched a lift up the long hill out of town with the old fruit and vegetable man on his horse and cart.

As they approached the farm on the coastal road, they could see the fields dipping down towards the cliffs like a patchwork quilt and several fishing boats far away in the distance.

In the field where they were harvesting, the clatter of the threshing machine filled the summer air. Jack went off along the hedgerow to look for blackberries, while Soggy settled on a pile of stones in the corner of the field to enjoy the warm sunshine.

He was just dozing off when he heard a very grumpy voice shout, "Oi, what are you doing in my field?"

Soggy was startled… and looking around he saw a hat and a long nose poking out of the corn.

He ran to get Jack as fast as he could.

When they returned, the voice, the nose and the hat had become a person... although quite a small and rather odd one.

Jack chuckled to himself and whispered, "I think he is supposed to be a scarecrow, Soggy!"

"Do you have a name, Sir?" Jack asked.

"You can call me Captain," he replied... pulling himself up to his full but not very great height.

"Are you a scarecrow?" Jack continued, looking at all the crows hopping happily amongst the corn.

"I am, unfortunately," the Captain replied.

"I hail from a seafaring background. I was Captain of a fine ship and searched for islands full of parrots and golden treasure. But my life has been one of storms and shipwreck, and I have had to take up employment ashore. I thought I was doing a good job… leastways I was until the field mice took my legs, which were made of straw, to build their nests. Now I cannot do my job properly because the crops grow higher than I stand. Worse than that, I can no longer see the ocean. Every day I hope that my old ship might appear over the horizon, full of golden treasure."

Soggy, having been frightened at first, now felt quite sorry for this little scarecrow, who was hardly bigger than himself.
He wondered if there were other crops he might stand guard over.

The Captain looked straight at Soggy and said, "I know what you are thinking, but I cannot do cabbages as they make me sneeze and I am unable to do carrots as I am afraid of rabbits. I refuse to do potato fields because they are for learner scarecrows only!"

"Well, Captain," Jack said, "you do seem to have a great many problems. Perhaps you should come home with us and talk to our Grandfather. He used to be at sea and might be able to help."
"I might as well," sighed the Captain, "I do not appear to be much use around here, with the summer almost over and the harvest nearly in."

They said their farewells to the farmer, who
did not mind his scarecrow leaving the job.
Just like the crows, the farmer had forgotten
he was there!

Soggy wondered how they were going to get the Captain home, as he obviously had trouble walking. But Jack said, "If we can get him down to the Island of Seals, Grandfather said earlier he would pick us up there to save the long walk home."

Jack and Soggy carried the Captain down the long path, across the fields to the Island of Seals. As he had promised, there was Grandfather, waiting to take them home in his boat.

Grandfather was most upset to see a fellow sailor in such
difficulties and vowed straight away to make him some new legs.

The Captain, for his part, was rather overwhelmed at being back on board a boat, even though it did not compare with the mighty vessels he had commanded in the past.

"Sit yourself down, Captain," said Grandfather when they got home. "I have just the wood for some seafarer's legs," he said, "and a fine pair of sea boots to go with them."

When the Captain's new legs were completed, Soggy and Jack helped him to practise walking, so he would be ready when the crops started growing in the spring, and the farmers would need experienced scarecrows.

In the long winter evenings, Grandfather and the Captain told tall tales of the Seven Seas.

Turquoise the mermaid, told fishy tales of life under the ocean.

Soggy's dreams were full of pirates and golden treasure.

When the sea was too rough for fishing, Grandfather spent his days out on the cliffs.

Jack and Soggy wondered what he was doing there, but Grandfather would only wink and say, "It's a surprise for the Captain."

One day when Jack got home from school, Grandfather told him that the Captain had left to start his new job.

"We will visit him at the weekend to see how he is getting on."

On the Saturday, after breakfast,
Soggy, Jack and Grandfather walked
out along the cliff path towards the great
rock called Man's Head.
Soggy remembered its distinctive shape very
well from when he was rescued from the sea.

Turquoise was waiting for them in a rock pool.

Jack carried her up the winding
path following Grandfather and
Soggy along the cliff edge with the sea
pounding the rocks below.
And there it was…

... the secret cliff-top garden that Grandfather's friend William tended so lovingly. Grandfather had been helping William transform it into an amazing place.

It was almost like a ship.
The fence was festooned with nets
and floats and ropes, and at the end of
a barnacled chain was a great anchor.
There was even a ship's mast and a
Captain's cabin full of cooing pigeons,

and there was the Captain... standing tall in a field of golden daffodils.

He greeted his friends with a big smile.
"I am once more Captain of a fine ship, and it is filled with nature's golden treasure."

"Welcome aboard, shipmates!"